TERRY DEARY

Footsteps in the Fog

D1343955

First published 2003 by
A & C Black Publishers Ltd
37 Soho Square, London, W1D 3QZ

www.acblack.com

Text copyright © 2003 Terry Deary
Illustrations copyright © 2003 Kathryn Baker

The rights of Terry Deary and Kathryn Baker to be identified as
author and illustrator of this work have been asserted by them
in accordance with the Copyrights, Designs and Patents Act 1988.

ISBN 0-7136-6573-4

A CIP catalogue for this book is available from the British Library.

A&C Black uses paper produced with elemental chlorine-free
pulp, harvested from managed sustained forests.

Printed and bound in Spain by G. Z. Printek, Bilbao.

TERRY DEARY

Footsteps in the Fog

Illustrated by
Kathryn Baker

A & C Black • London

For Mary Jones

Chapter One
Soft Steps, Soft Scarf

Soft footsteps followed the children through the fog. The morning fog swallowed sounds. No birds sang on that drear December day. Trees dripped their dampness on the pavement and hid the soft sound of the steps.

The boy and the girl were too busy talking to notice.

'What is green, grows in fields and is made of concrete?' Laura Lund asked as she hurried down the mist-muffled street to school.

Tommy Pickford's little legs were almost running to keep up with her. He screwed up his small nose in a frown. His watery eyes blinked behind big glasses. 'I don't know, Laura. What's green, grows in fields and is made of concrete?'

Laura grinned. 'Grass!'

Tommy stopped, stuck his hands deep into the pockets of his faded jacket and stared at the pavement. Somewhere in the fog the silent footsteps stopped. Suddenly Tommy's face split into a crooked grin. 'Hah! Hah! Hah! That's very funny, Laura.'

Laura stopped and sighed. 'No it's not, Tommy.'

He blinked again. 'Isn't it? I thought it was a joke.'

'You're supposed to say, "What about the concrete?"'

'Oh! What about the concrete?'

Laura chuckled. 'I just threw that in to make it hard!'

Tommy stared at the pavement. 'Did you?'

'Yes ... I mean, no. I mean that *is* the joke. You can laugh now, Tommy,' she urged.

'Hah! Hah! Hah!' the boy laughed weakly. He set off down the cold street again and turned into Meek Street. The footsteps followed. Finally Tommy said, 'I don't get it, Laura.'

Laura shook her head. Telling jokes to Tommy Pickford was like trying to stick pins in an elephant – very hard work and in the end he never got the point.

Tommy was shivering in his thin trousers and worn jacket.

'Want to try my new scarf?' Laura asked. She took off her blue scarf and wrapped it round his neck. It had white snowmen on with red noses and red hats.

Tommy stroked the fine wool and his eyes widened. 'Thanks, Laura. It's great.'

'It's an early Christmas present,' she explained. 'There's a pair of socks to match,' she told him and waved a leg in the air.

The thin boy's mouth fell open as he stared at the dark blue socks with the same snowman pattern. 'But you have to wear white socks,' he whispered. 'School rules. Mr Dixon will go mad.'

The girl shrugged and threw her head back. 'Old Dixon is mad. Anyway it's the last day of term and it's not like a proper school day. We'll be tidying up this morning – then there's the show this afternoon,' she said.

Tommy nodded glumly and the girl's face twitched with pain. 'Sorry, Tommy, I forgot your mum won't pay for you to go to the show.'

'It's all right,' the boy answered.

'I wish you'd let me pay for you. Since Dad won five million on the lottery I can afford a hundred tickets,' she cried. 'A thousand!'

Tommy shook his head. They'd had this argument before. 'Mum would kill me if she found out,' he said quietly. 'She says, "Lend your money and lose your friend."' Tommy frowned. 'I'm not sure what she means – but she says it's for my own good.'

'All right. Sorry,' Laura said.

They walked on towards the school gates in silence, each with their own thoughts. Suddenly Tommy said, 'So really you lied about the concrete.'

Laura laughed. 'That's right.'

'I believed you,' the boy said.

'That's your trouble, Tommy. You believe everything anyone tells you. It isn't good for you. You'd believe the moon was made of green cheese.'

He nodded.

'It's not, Tommy. Now, it's five to nine,' she went on looking at her watch. 'And we'll be late for school if we don't hurry – and that's the truth.'

Somewhere out of the mist a whistle cut the cold air and the playground noises faded from the street. Suddenly Tommy stumbled as he hurried after his friend. Looking down he saw the lace of his shoe was loose. 'You go on, Laura,' he said. 'I'll catch up later!' And she was gone.

His fingers were numb and fumbling in the cold and Tommy struggled with the laces. Silent steps on rubber-soled shoes moved closer. After two minutes of struggling Tommy heard a voice say, 'Can I help you, my young friend?'

Tommy looked up. Then he looked up again until his neck hurt. The man was very tall. His hair was wild and white as a dandelion seed and his eyes glowed like two grey globes. Tommy was afraid.

The man smiled a thin-lipped smile and knelt beside the boy. 'Here,' he offered. 'Let me do that.'

Tommy froze as the man's long, fine, grey fingers fastened the lace. His pale face was close to Tommy's now. 'Didn't your little girlfriend stop to help you, then?' he said and his voice was cold as the damp pavement.

'Late for school,' Tommy mumbled. Grown-ups made him shy. They usually ignored him. He didn't like speaking to them unless he had to. This grown-up was extra grown and extra scary.

'She seemed such a nice girl too. What is her name?' the man asked and the grey eyes looked through Tommy.

'Laura – Laura Lund,' he whispered.

The man nodded. 'Lund. Such an unusual name. Someone of that name won a fortune on the lottery not so long ago,' he said.

'Laura's dad,' Tommy croaked.

'Ah, yes. So that's the rich little Laura Lund, is it?' the man said and his eyes looked at where she had gone into the school. 'No doubt I'll see you both at the show this afternoon.'

'Are you going?' Tommy asked.

The man gave a curious smile. 'I am a guest. The show won't start without me. We'll have fun!'

Tommy shook his head and stood up. 'I can't afford it. Mum's saving up for a chicken for Christmas dinner,' he explained.

'Oh dear!' the man cried and stood up quickly.

Tommy wasn't sure what happened next. The man's hand twisted in the air and the fingers rippled like a nest of snakes. Suddenly a piece of white card appeared in the hand.

'There you are!' the man cried. 'One show ticket for this afternoon!' He leaned back as if waiting for the boy to applaud the trick.

But Tommy said, 'Won't you need it to get in?'

The man laughed. 'Oh, no. You take it, my boy.'

'Why?' Tommy said flatly.

'Because I like children. I like to make them happy,' he smiled.

And Tommy remembered something that Laura had told him. 'You believe everything anyone tells you. It isn't good for you.' He decided he didn't believe the tall grey man. Laura would be pleased.

The man's hand shot forward and slipped the ticket into Tommy's pocket. 'See you this afternoon,' he promised and he disappeared down the street on soft and almost silent shoes.

Tommy clutched his friend's blue scarf to his throat and ran into the school.

Chapter Two
Black Van, Magic Man

'It was magic!' Tommy squeaked as he told Laura his story.

'Tommy Pickford!' Mr Dixon bellowed. 'You do not talk in assembly! What do you not do in assembly?'

Tommy's mouth moved but no sounds would come out of his throat.

'Sorry, sir,' Laura said. 'It was my fault. I asked Tommy something.'

Mr Dixon smoothed his greasy, grey hair and his mean little eyes glowed behind his glasses. 'Come out to the front, Laura Lund,' he ordered.

Laura sighed and obeyed. The girl stood in front of the teacher. She put most of her weight on one foot, folded her arms and looked very bored. This made the teacher even more angry. Laura knew it would.

He spoke with a hiss. His voice was soft as last year's dust but it carried to the back of the hall. 'You are getting a little too big for your boots, Miss Lund,' he sneered.

Tommy scratched his head. He wondered how

Mr Dixon could tell that Laura's feet had grown!

'Yes, sir,' Laura said politely.

'You are heading for a nasty fall, young lady,' the teacher went on.

Tommy trembled. He couldn't bear the thought of Laura having a fall and hurting herself. Maybe Mr Dixon thought that Laura's big feet would trip her up.

'Yes, sir,' Laura sighed and looked as bored as a goldfish.

'You will come unstuck!' the teacher told her.

Now Tommy understood. Laura was becoming too big for her shoes so they would split. When the sole became unstuck she would trip over them and have a nasty fall! Never mind, he thought, there's some glue in the classroom. He'd soon fix them for his friend.

'Now,' the teacher was growling, 'get back to your place. One more peep out of you and you can wave goodbye to your seat at the show this afternoon.'

Tommy wondered why Laura would want to do that. She returned and sat down next to him with a *fffffflumppppp*. The girl winked at him and he managed a shy smile.

'We will now sing *While Shepherds Watched Their Flocks by Night*,' the teacher announced.

The pupils stood and Mrs Fattorini jangled out something on the piano that could have been *God Save the Queen*.

Tommy didn't usually sing the hymns in assembly. The words were hard for him to read. He just moved his mouth and made some sound. Sometimes Laura would whisper a line to him and he would join in. But this morning Laura was too busy singing at the top of her voice. And when Tommy heard the words his mouth fell open and he forgot to pretend to sing. He just listened.

'While shepherds washed their socks by night,' Laura roared.

'All seated round the tub!'

Slowly the class lowered their hymn books and raised their voices to join in.

'The angel of the Lord came down,
And gave them all a scrub!'

Mr Dixon turned pink, then purple. 'Stop! Stop! This is disgraceful. My class will return to their room. This morning will be spent doing one hundred sums. Dismiss!'

Laura shrugged. 'Didn't want to clean his mucky cupboards anyway,' she sniffed.

Tommy nodded. 'Mind you don't trip over your shoes,' he whispered.

'Eh?' Laura blinked. She shook her head and followed her friend into the classroom. Sometimes he was hard to understand.

The class worked in silence until break. The

bell rang and at last Laura was able to ask about Tommy's show ticket.

'I told you,' Tommy said as he huddled in a foggy corner near the school kitchen where the wall was warm. 'It was magic. The man made the ticket appear out of thin air.'

Laura pulled her snowman socks up and frowned. 'There's no such thing as magic, Tommy. Remember what I told you on the way to school?'

'You said I shouldn't believe everything people tell me.'

'Hmm. And you shouldn't believe everything you see, either,' she warned.

'So how did he make the ticket appear?' he asked.

'Probably had it tucked up his sleeve,' the girl explained. 'That's the way magicians do it.'

Tommy shook his head. 'But, Laura, he can't keep everything up his sleeve. He didn't know I wanted a ticket, did he?'

'No-o,' Laura said. 'But there must be a sensible reason for what happened.'

She was just going to give some of her reasons when Mr Dixon appeared in the yard and began shouting. 'Stand back! Out of the way. Stand back I said, you stupid boy! Out of the way! Clear the yard!'

Tommy peered around the corner of the

kitchen wall and saw a large black van reversing into the yard. It was backing up to the door that led on to the school stage. Excited children were crowding round and trying to look into the cab.

The van was old – like something you'd see in a museum. Clouds of blue smoke billowed into the misty air. Big round headlamps glowed on the thin black mudguards. Tommy thought the van had a face – the lamps were the eyes and the bumper bar was a smiling serpent's mouth.

There was a bright green flash in flaking paint on the flat sides of the van. The flash was surrounded by fading silver stars and scratched moons. Right across it was a long word in peeling pink letters.

'What does it say?' Tommy asked.

Laura peered into the gloom and read it. 'Marvello. It must be the magician setting up for this afternoon's show.'

Tommy nodded. He wanted to join the excited group of children who were crowding round the cab of the van.

Mr Dixon was at the passenger door and opened it politely as soon as the van stopped. He held up a hand and helped a short, pretty girl to step down. Her smile was warm enough to melt the fog. It certainly melted Mr Dixon's frosty face.

'Welcome to Meek Street Primary School,' he grinned like a sick sheep. He seemed to hold her hand long after she was safely on the ground. 'Do-oo-oo come into the staffroom for a coffee,' he gurgled and led the way to the door.

Most of the children followed the teacher and the pretty girl and pressed their noses against the glass doors to get a better view.

So only Laura and Tommy saw the driver of the van as he stepped silently into the yard and began to unload it.

He was tall and thin and pale and dressed in a shiny black suit.

'That'll be Marvello,' Laura said and nudged the boy.

But Tommy was standing as stiff as a school-dinner scone. He was staring at the man's wispy white hair and big, bulging eyes. At last he squeaked, 'That's the man who gave me the ticket, Laura. It's the magic man!'

Chapter Three
Mind Game, Secret Name

After they'd eaten Christmas dinner, the hall was cleared of the tables. The smell of turkey hung in the air.

'My turkey was tough,' Martin Minto moaned.

'Lucky you,' Laura Lund laughed. 'My gravy was tough!'

They giggled and went on arranging the chairs to face the stage. Tommy shook his head. His turkey was the tastiest meal he'd had all year – though the pudding sat in his stomach like a bag of marbles.

The pupils trooped in. Mr Dixon stood on the stage in the school hall and glared at the children. The buzz of excitement died.

'Now then, children, this afternoon we have our special Christmas treat – James Wood, stop chewing, boy, you're not at home now – we have brought you a famous magician ... the mystical and mind-boggling Marvello! I'm sure that you have all seen him on the television ...'

'Ye-es, Mis-ter Dix-on,' two hundred voices cried.

'I haven't got a television,' Tommy whispered.

'It doesn't matter,' Laura shrugged. 'He isn't all that famous or he wouldn't be performing in Meek Street Primary. Mum says he's past it now.'

'Past what?' Tommy asked.

'Past ... well, past ... *it*!' Laura said with a shake of her head.

Mr Dixon was droning on. 'The famous Mr Marvello was telling me in the staffroom about the time when he was almost invited to perform for Her Royal Highness Queen Elizabeth II!'

'Ooooh!' the pupils gasped.

Mr Dixon gave a smug smile. 'So, I hope you are all going to be on your very best behaviour ...'

'Ye-es, Mis-ter Dix-on.'

'I hope you will sit quietly and pay attention – stop coughing, Linda Ridley – that's the last thing Marvello wants to hear ... and I hope you will clap politely for all of his tricks.'

'Ye-es, Mis-ter Dix-on.'

The teacher lifted his chin, stuck out his chest like a turkey and said, 'I am very proud to welcome to Meek Street Primary School the great Marvello! Put the spotlights on, Mrs Fattorini!'

Mr Dixon stepped down from the stage and

sat, smiling, at the side of the hall. The hall lights went off and the spotlights came on. They lit the faded, red stage curtains with a new glow that promised magic.

There was a pause. Slowly the curtains jerked open, stuck, then jerked a little wider open.

On stage stood a table covered with odd objects in boxes. Behind was a screen decorated like the side of the magician's black van.

There was a sharp click, a scratchy hiss, then the tinny sound of a cheap tape-recorder playing dramatic music. Marvello stepped on to the stage. He was covered from neck to toe in a black cloak with a purple satin lining. His globe-eyes glittered in the spotlights.

'Welcome to the world of magic and mystery,' he cried above the crackling tape.

'The world of fake and fraud,' Laura Lund sniffed. She wrinkled her nose and shook her head. 'Don't believe everything you see, Tommy. Remember that.'

'I won't, Laura.'

After a few waves of Marvello's thin, pale hands, packs of cards appeared, which he dropped into a top hat. He turned the hat upside down. Now it was empty. The children gasped. Marvello plunged his hand into the hat and pulled out a rainbow-string of coloured scarves.

'It's a trick hat,' Laura whispered to Tommy whose mouth had fallen open.

'I wish I had one,' Tommy sighed.

'To do silly tricks?'

'No. To keep my head dry,' the boy told her.

'And now,' Marvello cried, 'let me introduce to you my lovely assistant, the Adorable Alice!'

The pretty girl who had been in the van now stepped on to the stage. The children gasped and James Wood was about to whistle until Mr Dixon caught his eye. Alice was dressed in a glittering costume of red and orange that sparkled in the spotlights. She perched on very high heels and smiled warmly at the audience.

The Adorable Alice's main job seemed to be to fetch and carry for Marvello as he ran through his tricks. Card tricks with children from the audience and making coins appear from their ears and noses. Rabbits popped out from under Marvello's cloak and even from under a handkerchief.

Tommy watched closely but couldn't see how the tricks were done. The children soon forgot Mr Dixon's order to be quiet and polite. They roared when the Adorable Alice stepped off the stage, took the teacher by the hand and led him into the spotlight.

They cheered when Marvello set light to Mr Dixon's ten-pound note and smashed his wrist-watch with a hammer. They laughed when the Adorable Alice slipped a hand inside the teacher's jacket and giggled at his blushes as the girl pulled out the watch and ten-pound note as good as new.

But the children fell silent when Marvello ordered the lights to be dimmed. They faded to a yellow glow and only a little grey light from the foggy yard spilled into the hall and on to Tommy's worried face.

'Why did he do that?' he asked softly.

His friend sniffed. 'So you can't see what he's up to. He's going to try and pull the wool over our eyes.'

'I can't see any wool,' Tommy said as he peered at the dim stage.

Marvello was pushing a long box on stage. Each end rested on a trolley.

'Has he got a sheep in the box?' Tommy asked.

'A what?'

'A sheep. To pull its wool over our eyes.'

Laura sighed and muttered, 'Just watch and see.'

'I will now ask the Adorable Alice to step into the box!' Marvello cried.

The girl smiled brightly and climbed carefully into a box like a coffin. The magician closed the coffin and left the Adorable Alice's head sticking out of one end.

'I want you to put your feet through the holes in the end of the box,' the man in the cape ordered his assistant. Two feet in high-heeled shoes popped out of the end of the coffin. 'Now place your hands through the holes in the side.'

Alice waved a hand at the audience.

Marvello walked to the edge of the stage and took a large saw from the dark corner. 'I will now cut the Adorable Alice in half,' he told the children.

'He can't do that!' Tommy squeaked.

Laura clicked her tongue. 'Don't believe everything you see,' she said. 'That's Alice's head at the top and her hands at the side – but it's someone else's feet at the bottom. Alice is cramped into the top half of the coffin – the other girl is squashed into the bottom half. He'll cut between them, just you see.'

Tommy nodded and watched as the magician swept through the coffin with the saw. Suddenly he said. 'Who?'

Laura blinked. 'Who what?'

'Who's in the bottom half?' Tommy asked.

'Another assistant,' Laura said impatiently.

'But he only came with one,' Tommy reminded her.

The girl frowned in the dim light and said, 'She must have been hiding.'

Tommy nodded. The magician pulled the two halves of the coffin apart to cheers from the children. Then he joined them together again, said some magic words and let the Adorable Alice out of the box ... all in one piece. As the girl took a bow Mr Dixon was cheering more wildly than anyone.

Marvello waved a hand for silence as Alice pushed the two halves of the coffin off the stage. 'Now we will show you a feat of mind-reading.'

'Ooooh!' the audience gasped.

'The Adorable Alice will move into the audience ... while I turn my back on you.'

The magician's helper moved into the audience, still smiling. 'Stop!' Marvello commanded.

Alice stopped at the end of Tommy's row.

'Will the second child along please stand up.'

It was Laura. Laura stood up. Even in that dim light Tommy thought he could see his friend turn pale.

'Alice ... I want you to place your hand on that child's head,' the magician said.

Alice reached across Tommy and he could smell her sweet, cheap perfume.

'Now, child,' the magician cried. 'I want you to think of your name ... your thought will travel into the mind of the Adorable Alice, through the air and into my mind by magic. Now,' he ordered. 'Think!'

Laura closed her eyes and thought hard. The man on the stage raised his arms in the air. 'I see a girl's name ... you are a girl?'

Laura looked worried. 'Yes, but ...'

'And I see the letter "L" ... I see two "L"s ... LL! Are your initials L.L.?'

'Yes, but ...'

'And I feel you are telling me your name is Laura ... Laura Lund! Am I correct?'

'Yes, but ...'

Laura's words were drowned by a cheer of amazement from the children in the hall.

Marvello turned round and his globe eyes shone brighter than Alice's sequins. 'Come on stage, Laura Lund ... as a special treat you can be part of my last and greatest trick.'

Alice took Laura's hand. The girl stumbled over Tommy as she left the row of seats. 'How did he know?' she whispered.

'He read your mind,' Tommy said.

'But my mind was thinking of someone else's name ... I thought of your name, Tommy!' Laura hissed as Alice almost dragged her past Tommy. 'Someone must have told him before the show!' she said over her shoulder as she was marched towards the stage.

Tommy felt a hand as cold as the December fog clutch at his heart. 'I did, Laura,' he murmured to himself. 'I did.'

And he felt afraid.

Chapter Four

Magic Box, Blue Socks

'Ladies and gentlemen, boys and girls!' Marvello cried. 'The cupboard is completely empty,' he went on, pointing to the black box, like a wardrobe, that Alice wheeled on to the stage.

He rapped the sides with his wand. 'A solid cupboard. A cupboard with no secret compartments or trapdoors.' He smiled. 'Would someone like to examine the cupboard?'

About a hundred children jumped to their feet and waved hands in the air crying, 'Please, sir! Me, sir! Please, sir!'

But Mr Dixon was on his feet and snapping, 'Sit down! Sit down! Quiet! Sit down!'

Alice smiled her most charming smile and stretched out a hand to the teacher. Mr Dixon blushed again and followed the adorable assistant on to the stage. He poked the box, prodded it and rapped it. Finally he said, 'Just an ordinary cupboard!'

Marvello swished his purple-lined cloak and cried, 'My good sir, would you stay on the stage and keep a close eye on what happens? No tricks

... just pure magic!' The magician took Laura's hand. 'Step into the cupboard, young Laura.'

Laura's eyes met Tommy's. They were frightened eyes. It seemed to the boy that the magician had to drag Laura into the cupboard.

He slammed the door quickly and swept his huge cloak over it. After a lot of waving of the magic wand, and mumbling magic words, the tall man finally opened the door again.

The cupboard was empty.

The children gasped. Mr Dixon looked around the back of the cupboard, squinted inside it and even looked underneath. He shook his head in amazement.

The magician pointed his wand at Mrs Fattorini. 'Turn your spotlight on the door!' he commanded.

Mrs Fattorini swung the spotlight round till it pointed to the doors at the back of the hall. 'Are you there, Laura Lund?' Marvello roared. Everyone in the hall swung round to look.

The curtains parted. Tommy and the children had a brief glimpse of a girl in Meek Street Primary uniform. A smile, a wave, then the curtains closed again and the girl had gone. Tommy glanced back at the stage in time to see Alice and Mr Dixon wheeling the cupboard off the stage and straight towards the side doors where the van waited.

'Yes!' the magician laughed. 'That is true magic!' He began to speak very quickly as Alice returned to tidy the stage and a sweating Mr Dixon slipped back into his seat at the side. 'We hope you have all enjoyed the show and that you all have a very happy holiday. Farewell from me and from the Adorable Alice!'

The children cheered and clapped as the curtains creaked closed. They shouted for more, but the stage was silent and the hall lights went on. The head teacher made a quick speech of thanks and sent the children home with a warning to be careful when crossing the roads in the fog.

The hall emptied in record time. Only Tommy Pickford sat alone, clutching at Laura's blue scarf. 'Don't believe everything you see,' he muttered and his thin face creased in a frown. 'I don't believe Laura vanished into thin air,' he said firmly. That made him feel a little better. 'So it must have been a trick cupboard!' he decided. 'And I don't believe it was Laura at the back of the hall.'

Then he remembered something. 'Mr Dixon said it wasn't a trick cupboard!' But Laura had told him not to believe everything he heard. 'So Mr Dixon was wrong.'

'Why haven't you gone home?' the teacher's voice said and Tommy jumped. Mr Dixon was standing in the doorway wearing an overcoat and leather gloves.

'I'm waiting for Laura,' Tommy muttered.

'She must have gone straight home,' the teacher told him.

Tommy shook his head. 'She hasn't come off the stage yet.'

The teacher walked towards the boy and leaned over him. 'She was at the back of the hall. You saw her with your own two eyes. She went straight home from the back of the hall.'

'She wouldn't go without me,' Tommy argued.

Mr Dixon's eyes were big as saucers behind the thick glasses. His hair oil smelled like dead flowers. 'You saw her with your own two eyes.'

But Tommy shook his head. 'I saw someone in Meek Street School uniform,' he said carefully. 'Navy blazer, blue sweatshirt, grey skirt and white socks.'

'Laura Lund!'

'Laura wasn't wearing school socks today,' Tommy insisted. 'She was wearing blue socks with snowmen on them.'

The teacher looked hard at the boy. 'Very clever, Tommy Pickford. Pity you aren't as clever as that in class tests. Your miserable scores pull my whole class average down. How do you think I feel about that?'

Tommy shook his head silently.

'I'm ashamed to have an idiot like you in my room.'

Tears pricked at Tommy's eyes. He sniffed. 'I'm just not very good at reading,' he mumbled.

'Get out, Pickford. Laura Lund went straight home. I saw her myself,' the teacher snarled and stepped back.

Tommy rose to his feet. With a last look back at the darkened stage he trudged out of the hall and into the misty night. He tugged at the blue scarf. 'I'll take this back to Laura,' he said. 'See if she's really all right!'

And his feet slapped softly on the wet pavement. He didn't hear the silent footsteps that followed him.

Chapter Five

Dark Park, Nonsense Note

Tommy tapped on the door of Laura's house. Mrs Lund was small and pretty and very like Laura. Still, he was almost too scared to speak. 'Is Laura home, Mrs Lund, please?'

She shook her head. 'Isn't she with you? I've only just had a phone call from your mother, Tommy. Asked if it was OK for Laura to stay at your house for tea.'

'Mum's at work till six o'clock,' Tommy mumbled, but Mrs Lund didn't seem to hear him.

A small frown crossed Mrs Lund's face. 'I wish Laura had told me before she went to school this morning.' Then her face brightened again. 'Didn't you go home from school with her?'

'I missed her at the end of the show,' Tommy explained.

Mrs Lund nodded. 'That's what's happened, then. She must have gone straight to your home. Tell her not to be too late!'

Tommy nodded dumbly. He hadn't agreed to take Laura home for tea. But if he told Mrs Lund that Laura was missing, she would worry. He had to check first.

The door closed. The boy clutched the scarf at his neck. 'I forgot to give her the scarf!' he muttered. He reached for the door bell then changed his mind. Perhaps Laura would be in trouble for lending Tommy her new scarf and forgetting it. He turned and walked down the misty street. His feet slapped quickly on the damp pavement as he hurried home. It was all wrong!

The park was cold and quiet. No one was playing football here tonight. He put his head down and tried to forget the dark shapes that loomed out of the fog. They were only bushes. And those soft sounds weren't really footsteps following him. They were just drops of dampness falling from the black-twigged trees on to the path below.

The Parkside Flats glowed as warm and welcoming as a lighthouse when he reached the other side of the park. But Tommy shivered with fear.

The lift was broken as it usually was. He ran up seven flights of stairs until his chest hurt with the effort.

The door to his flat was locked. The lights were out. He unlocked it and pushed the door open.

'Laura?' he called. The flat was cold and empty.

He found a pencil in his pocket and an old shopping list on the kitchen table. On the back he struggled to write …

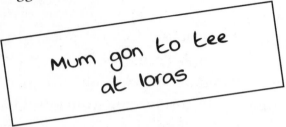

Mum gon to tee at loras

… and hoped she'd understand his writing.

Ten minutes later Tommy stepped out of the door.

Somebody had taken the bulb out of the landing light again. He could hear the sound of his own breathing in the darkness. He could smell the sour pickle and stale cabbage smell that the flats always had. And there was also a curious perfume smell this evening.

For some reason he felt he had to tiptoe along the landing. Every step he took was followed by the creak of a floorboard.

Step … creak. Step … creak. Step … creak.

He stopped.

The echoes didn't!

Creak … creak … creak!

There was someone else out there in the thick dark.

He groped for the banister rail and felt it: cold metal, chipped paint. Suddenly he threw

38

himself down the steep stairs, three at a time, flight after flight, till he reached the safety of the amber street lights below.

Fog rolled in across the park. It crept through his thin jacket and made him shiver. Still, it felt good to be out in the open. And as the fog was hiding the park trees it could hide him.

He looked back into the dark doorway.

There was a shadow moving in that shadow ...

Tommy hurried towards the park gate. There was a man standing there. A tall, thin man dressed in black. He was trying to read a newspaper under the dim street lamp. Tommy felt as if the man were waiting for him.

He turned back to the door to the flats and the shadow moved towards him. As the figure moved out into the light of the street, Tommy sighed with relief. It was a harmless old lady.

The woman shuffled towards him, her face hidden by a dark headscarf. 'Here, boy!' the voice creaked. 'You're Tommy Pickford, aren't you?'

Tommy nodded.

'I have a message for you from your friend, Laura Lund,' the woman went on.

She fumbled in her pocket and pulled out a piece of paper. Tommy could smell the sickly-sweet perfume of the woman as she held the paper towards him.

'Where is she?' he asked. 'Is she all right?'

'It's all in the letter,' the woman said and turned to shuffle down the street. The man across the road folded his newspaper and slowly followed the old woman.

Tommy's brain was racing. He knew the man had followed him through the park. He knew the woman had been waiting for him to come out of his flat and she had followed him down the stairs. Between them they had trapped him like a hunted fox.

'Don't believe everything you see,' Laura had warned him.

And the boy knew that the woman wasn't old. She was young and pretty but acting old.

She had hidden her face and changed her voice ... but she hadn't had time to change her smell. She wore the cheap perfume of the Adorable Alice.

'Don't believe everything you hear,' Laura had said.

And Tommy knew that they were lying when they said that Laura had written him this message. Because Laura knew about his trouble with reading. Laura would never send a message that way.

As the man and the woman faded into the fog at the end of the street, Tommy saw them come together. The woman shook off the scarf and seemed to shake off forty years in age.

Tommy, the hunted fox, clutched at the blue scarf at his neck. He decided it was time he became the hunter. Keeping to the shadows of doorways he set off after the Adorable Alice ... and the man who could only be the mad-eyed Marvello.

Chapter Six

Battered Bike, Cop Drop

The two people turned a corner and walked towards a dark shape at the side of the road. Tommy lost sight of them for a moment and ran till his thin legs were shaking. The boy's heart sank.

The magician and his assistant were climbing into a van. A black van with a green flash and silver moons and stars. There was a pink word on the side of the van. Tommy knew it said 'Marvello'.

The van started up in a cloud of blue exhaust smoke. Tommy ran to the back and jumped on to a step; he clung on to the handle of the back door.

Tommy's hands soon turned numb with the cold and started to ache. His glasses began to slip down his nose as the van rattled along. He didn't dare take a hand off the van to push them back.

Luckily the fog was so thick the van was forced to crawl along. When it neared the town centre the bright shop lights made driving easier and the van began to speed up.

Tommy's hand started to slip. He looked down at the rushing ground and prepared to fall. He knew it was going to hurt. Just as one hand finally slipped off the handle the van began to slow and stopped sharply.

Traffic lights showed red. Cars full of families going shopping pulled up behind the van. Children stared and pointed at Tommy. Tommy took the chance to push his glasses back on to his nose. He rubbed his hands to warm them then pulled out a handkerchief from his pocket. Just as he was wrapping it around the cold handle a shadow fell across the van door. A stern voice said, 'And what's going on here?'

Tommy looked round quickly. A young policeman, thin as a navy-coloured pencil with silver buttons, glared at him. The policeman sat on a bicycle in the traffic and demanded, 'What's your game, my lad?'

'My what?' Tommy trembled.

'I said, what is your game?'

'Well, it's football in the winter and cricket in the summer,' Tommy explained.

At that moment the traffic lights changed to green and the van jerked forward. Tommy grabbed at the handle. The policeman's long legs whirred round as he set off after the van. 'Hey! What are you doing?' he cried.

Tommy thought that was a daft question but he answered politely. 'I'm hanging on to the back of this van!'

'I can see that!' the P.C. panted. 'I meant why are you hanging on to it?'

'Because, if I didn't hang on, I'd fall off,' the boy explained.

The policeman moved up a gear and sped after the van. He was catching up quickly now. He was almost close enough to touch the boy when the van reached the next set of traffic lights. They were on red. The cyclist couldn't see the lights for the van. That was why he ran slap into the back bumper when the van stopped.

As he shot over the handlebars his head

crunched into the back door. His helmet saved his head. He tumbled back on to the tangled wreck of his bike and groaned. Sooty smoke from the van choked him and a broken cycle spoke poked him in the ear. He staggered to his feet and reached for Tommy as the van pulled away. The policeman jumped on to the back step and clutched at the boy. 'Now then,' he gasped, 'I'll have to ask you to accompany me.'

Tommy shrugged. 'I haven't got a piano.'

'Eh?' The young policeman blinked.

'Mr Dixon tells Mrs Fattorini to "accompany" us when we sing in assembly,' Tommy explained. 'But she has a piano.'

The man shouted over the rumble of the van. 'I mean, accompany me to the station!'

'Are we going to catch a train?' Tommy asked.

'The police station!' the man roared. 'I'll have to charge you!'

'But I can't afford to pay!' Tommy trembled.

'Pay? Pay what?'

'I can't afford to pay the charge,' the boy sighed.

The policeman shook his head and his crumpled helmet fell over his eyes. He raised a hand to move it and began to fall backwards. He snatched for the back of the door and caught hold of one of the door handles.

The handle dropped as he grabbed it and the

door swung open. Tommy saw his chance. He grabbed the edge of the open door and pulled himself into the back of the van where he lay panting and stiff.

Moments later, the policeman hauled himself in too. He stepped on Tommy, tripped and fell into the back. When he crunched his head into a heavy box his broken helmet didn't save him this time. He was knocked out colder than a duck's foot.

The van squealed to a stop. The two front doors slammed and Tommy heard voices. Angry voices, arguing voices.

'How could you be so stupid?' Marvello the magician was saying.

'It was dark and foggy. I got the notes mixed up,' a whining woman's voice replied.

'So,' Marvello sighed, 'you gave the boy the note we wrote for the girl's parents! Hah! I wonder what he makes of that?'

'He won't make anything of it,' the girl sniffled. 'He looked too dim to read it, never mind understand it.'

'I hope you're right,' the man said in a menacing growl.

Then Tommy heard footsteps coming to the back of the van. He glanced out and saw they had left the bright lights of the town centre behind now. He crouched in the shadow of a long, black box.

'The back door's come open,' the girl said. 'This van is a wreck. I told you we should get a new one.'

'Hah! By the time we collect the ransom we can afford a hundred new vans,' the man cackled. 'Let's just lock it for now and see what the Boss wants us to do with the girl.'

Tommy saw the door close, heard keys rattle in the lock and the faint footsteps fading into the foggy night.

The van smelled of rabbits and musty material.

Somewhere in the dark a young policeman snored. And, from somewhere else in the dark, came a soft tapping and scrabbling like a rat in a box.

Chapter Seven

Gagged Laura, P.C. Snorer

Tommy squinted into the dark corners of the van. The old twisted doors let in a trickle of light. The boy could just make out the sleeping policeman – and a long, black wooden cupboard.

The tapping was coming from that cupboard. He peered through his glasses at it. Then he remembered it was the magic cupboard that Marvello had used on stage. The magic cupboard that had made Laura disappear!

There was another sound coming from the cupboard now. A muffled but urgent crying. 'Nnng! Nnng! Nnng!'

'Laura!' Tommy whispered, as he scrabbled at the catch on the door. 'You didn't vanish from the cupboard after all. I knew it wasn't you at the back of the hall! You never left the cupboard!'

He tore the door open and reached inside to help his best friend out. His knuckles scraped painfully against the rough, bare wood. He groped around desperately. But the cupboard was empty.

Still, the 'Nnng! Nnng! Nnng!' noises seemed to be coming from it. 'Don't believe everything you see,' he muttered. 'I see an empty cupboard ... but I don't believe it,' he muttered.

He closed his eyes and felt the edges of the cupboard. Then he felt the corners where the sides met the back of the cupboard. 'Nnng! Nnng! Nnng!'

'Don't worry, Laura. I'll find you,' he said. And he felt a small metal catch. It took him a minute or two to work it out, but Tommy was good with his hands. At last it opened with a soft click. The back of the cupboard sprang open to show a secret compartment. And in that compartment lay Laura Lund. A rainbow scarf from the magic act was wrapped around her mouth. Another scarf bound her hands and feet. It took the boy just a few moments to tear them off.

'Laura!' he cried. 'Are you all right?'

She wrapped her arms around him and hugged his thin body till his bones cracked. 'Tommy! You rescued me. You're just like Superman!' she laughed. 'Let's get out of here and fetch the police!'

'No, wait,' the boy said softly. 'We're locked in the back of Marvello's van ... and I've sort of brought a policeman with me.'

'Where?' Laura asked as she rubbed her stiff arms.

'He's asleep at the moment. Had a little accident,' and Tommy explained all that had happened since Laura vanished into the cupboard.

'You rode on the back of the van? All the way through the town?' the girl said as she hugged him again. 'You're not like Superman at all,' she grinned. 'You're better.'

Tommy wanted to change the subject. He felt his blushing cheeks must be glowing even in that darkness. 'I think I know how they trapped you. They used the trick cupboard and sent the other girl to wave from the back of the hall.'

'Dressed in a Meek Street uniform – they spent a lot of time planning this,' Laura said.

'But why did they do it, Laura? And why did they come to my flat and tell me you were all right?' Tommy murmured.

Laura nodded. 'You were the only one who spotted the switch. The only one who could warn the police before they were ready to go on with the plan ...'

'No!' Tommy objected. 'How did they know I'd spotted the switch?'

'You said you told Mr Dixon,' Laura reminded him. 'Maybe Marvello was hanging around and overheard.'

'Hmm,' Tommy nodded. 'So why did they do it?'

'I think the note will tell you that,' Laura said. 'They gave you a note meant for my mum and dad. I could hear them talking from inside the cupboard. Where is it now?'

'In my pocket,' the boy said and pulled the crumpled sheet from his anorak.

Laura took it and held it to the crack in the door. She read it slowly:

Dear Mr and Mrs Lund,

We have kidnapped your daughter.

Pay one million pounds into
Royal Bank account number
24682468. When the money is paid
in then we will let Laura go.

But beware. If you don't pay –
or if you tell the police –
then you will not see her ever
again. Just one million pounds.
You can afford it.

Laura nodded. 'They heard about Dad winning five million on the lottery,' she said. 'It was a good plan, but they reckoned without my friend Tommy Pickford. They don't know the boot's on the other foot now.'

'Have you changed them?' Tommy asked.

'Changed what, Tommy?'

'Changed your boots!'

Laura sighed. 'I mean ... I mean they don't know that we are now in control.'

'We're still trapped,' Tommy pointed out.

'They'll have to come for me soon – and when they do they'll find the police already waiting!'

53

'But he's knocked out.'

'Have to sort that out,' the girl said briskly and shook the policeman. 'Wake up!'

The man groaned, and struggled to sit up. 'Where am I?' he asked.

'In the back of Marvello's van. Don't you remember?'

'Remember what?'

'Where you are.'

'Where am I?'

'In the back of ... oh never mind,' Laura groaned. 'Do you know who you are?'

'Laurence Olivier,' the man said promptly.

Laura frowned. 'But Laurence Olivier was a famous actor.'

'I know. My mummy named me after him.

She called me Laurence Olivier Elloe,' he said.

Laura thought about this. 'L ... O ... Elloe?'

'Hello, L.O. Elloe,' Tommy laughed.

'Hello, hello, hello!' the man giggled. 'Hee! Hee! I sound just like a policeman.' Then he added, 'Mummy wants me to be an actor, just like Sir Laurence ... when I grow up.'

'When you what?' Laura gasped.

'Grow up!' the man replied happily. 'I'm only seven, you know?'

Tommy groaned. 'It must have been the knock on the head that did it!'

'He'll be no use to us in this state,' Laura hissed. 'Knock him on the head again!'

And the policeman burst into tears.

Chapter Eight
Boxed Boy, False Floor

'Have you got a torch?' Tommy asked P.C. Elloe.

The man patted his pockets as he sniffled miserably. Something rattled. He pulled out a box of matches.

'Strike one,' Laura ordered.

'Eeeeh! No!' the policeman gasped. 'Mummy doesn't let me play with matches.'

'I don't care what your mummy says. Strike a match or I'll strike you,' Laura snapped.

The man gave a small whimper and scratched the match against the side of the cupboard. Tommy looked around the van at the boxes and the baggage of the magician. Suddenly Laurence Elloe screeched, 'Yahhhh!' and dropped the match.

'What's wrong?' Tommy asked.

'There was a big, ugly policeman with a battered helmet staring at me!' the man said.

'That was a mirror,' Laura said patiently. 'You were looking at yourself! Now strike another match!'

The policeman's hands were shaking and he

spilled half the box before he managed to strike one. Tommy scooped the matches into his pocket while Laura looked around the van. 'Plenty of places to hide when they come,' she said.

Suddenly the policeman cried, 'Yahhhh!' again and dropped the second match.

'What's wrong now?' Laura groaned.

'I burnt me fingers,' the man whined. 'That's why Mummy doesn't let me play with matches!'

'Just pass them here,' Laura was saying when there was a soft click.

Outside, silent footsteps had walked to the back of the van and started to unlock it. Laura dived for a corner where she'd seen a 'saw-the-lady-in-half' box and crouched behind it. Tommy stumbled against the magic cupboard and fell into it. Springs clicked. First the secret panel slammed closed behind him, then the outside lid closed. He was trapped like a parrot in a cage ... but ten times as quiet.

In the silence he heard the van door creak open. Then Marvello gasped at the sight of the policeman, recovered and said, 'Who are you?'

'I'm a little teapot, short and stout!' P.C. Elloe giggled.

'Look at his helmet. He's had a knock on the head,' Marvello sneered. 'Put him in the room where we're keeping the girl,' he ordered. 'We'll ask the Boss what to do with him later.'

'OK, Marvello,' Alice, his assistant, said. 'Come on, Constable. Give me your hand.'

'Here's my handle,' the policeman laughed as he gave his hand to Alice. 'Here's my spout,' he added as he jumped out of the van.

A minute later there was a soft tap on the door. Laura hissed, 'I'll be back with the police in a few minutes, Tommy. Don't worry!'

He heard her scuffle from the van and her running footsteps fade. Tommy felt scared and alone. 'Laura told me not to worry,' he reminded himself and felt better.

There was silence for two minutes. Then Tommy heard Marvello say, 'Grab this end of the cupboard and we'll carry it in.'

He felt the cupboard rocking and bumping as it was carried into a building. The cupboard crunched against walls as it swung round corners and it tilted sharply as it was carried down steep stairs. Finally it was put down on its back with a bump.

'Shall we let her out?' Alice asked.

'No! We'll wait till the Boss gets here, then get another note to her parents,' the magician said.

Tommy heard two sets of footsteps leave the room. The door closed and the door lock clicked.

Then ... *bump!* Someone flopped on top of the magic box. A man's voice sang, 'Humpty Dumpty sat on a wall!'

There was a *flump!* as he fell off the cupboard on to the floor.

'Humpty Dumpty had a great fall!' P.C. Elloe giggled.

'Constable!' Tommy called.

'Ooooh! A talking box!'

'Open the door!' the boy said. He heard the outside door swing open.

'Ooooh! A magic box! Nobody in! A talking cupboard!' the policeman gasped.

'I'm underneath the back of the cupboard,' Tommy said.

'Ooooh!'

'There's a small catch at the top right hand corner,' Tommy explained. It was cramped under there and he felt he would suffocate if he didn't get out soon. What was that stupid man doing?

'Which side is the right side?' the policeman asked.

'You write with your right,' the boy in the box said and hoped the policeman wasn't left-handed.

'Ooooh! A little button!' the man said. His voice was very close now. He must have put his head right inside the cupboard.

'Press it!' Tommy called urgently.

There was a *click* as the catch opened, a *swoosh* as the false back swung open ... then a *splatttt* as it hit the poor policeman in the face.

'Ohhhh!' the constable groaned. 'Where am I?'

'You're a prisoner of Marvello the Magician!' Tommy said.

The policeman rubbed his head, felt his battered helmet and glared at Tommy. 'Is this a joke?'

'No!' Tommy said.

'The last thing I remember was climbing into the back of a moving van,' the man muttered.

Tommy nodded. The whack in the face with the magic cupboard had brought his memory back. Tommy quickly explained what had been happening.

P.C. Elloe straightened his shoulders. 'Kidnapping is bad enough,' he said. 'But kidnapping an officer of the law is the worst. The first person to walk through that door will be arrested!'

'Hmm,' the boy said. 'But if I was the kidnapper, and if I opened that door, and if I saw you ready to arrest me ... I'd lock it quick and run away.'

'Good thinking, son,' the policeman said. 'I'll hide behind the door, then. Wait till they're in, then grab them,' he suggested.

'Great idea,' Tommy smiled.

The policeman looked around the room. 'We seem to be in a boiler room under some big building. Where are we *exactly*?'

Tommy shrugged. 'I don't know. I was trapped in the box when they brought me out of the van. We could be anywhere.'

P.C. Elloe fiddled with his pocket radio. It was cracked and lifeless. 'Never mind. The gang will have been in touch with the girl's parents by now. They should be back soon to see if she's all right.'

And at that moment, as if he had seen through a window in the door, a key rattled in the lock. The policeman leapt to the top step and jumped behind the door. Tommy sat on the lid of the magic box and waited.

The door seemed to stick a little as the man on the other side pushed. That was why it opened with a jerk and flew out of Marvello's hand. That was how it clattered into the policeman who was hiding behind it.

Marvello's bulbous eyes glowed like an angry bull when he saw Tommy. 'How did you get here?' he snarled.

His assistant, dressed in black jeans and sweater, now looked past the magician's arm. 'Who are you?' she cried.

And from behind the door came the answer, 'I'm a little teapot, short and stout.'

Chapter Nine
Tables Turned, Tale Told

Tommy groaned. The slamming door had knocked the policeman senseless again.

The magician ignored P.C. Elloe and stepped into the room. 'It's Laura Lund's little idiot friend,' he explained to his assistant. 'She was in that box,' he snarled at Tommy. 'How did you get into a locked room?'

Tommy shrugged. 'Magic.'

The man gave Tommy a savage push out of his way and stood over the box. 'Where is she?'

That was when Alice stepped forward to look into the box – and left the way to the door clear.

Tommy dashed forward.

'Stop him!' Marvello roared. But Tommy grabbed P.C. Elloe's limp arm and tugged him into the path of Alice. As she tangled with the policeman and Marvello blundered into them both, Tommy rushed through the door. His brain was working at full speed. He stopped. He slammed the door shut behind him and noticed that the key was still in the lock. He twisted it quickly and gasped with joy as he heard his prisoners beat against it helplessly.

He found himself in a narrow passage. The sign on the locked door said 'Boiler Room'. He turned and climbed a concrete stairway and opened a door at the top. There was very little light – just some spilling from the street lights. But Tommy knew at once where he was. He knew the smell. He would have known it with his eyes closed.

He was standing in the entrance hall to Meek Street Primary School. He ran over to the glass front doors and pushed. They were locked, and this time there was no key.

He trotted through the deserted school to the side door beside his classroom. It led out into the school yard. That was locked too. He couldn't believe he'd escaped from the magic box and escaped from the locked room only to be trapped inside his school.

Tommy slipped into his own classroom and hurried over to the window. He tugged at the metal catch and the window swung open. The boy squeezed through and dropped on to the ground. As he raced around the corner of the school yard he collided heavily with a man in a grey overcoat.

'Oooof!' the man gasped and stepped back. 'You clumsy little brat!' He stepped back and glared at the boy. 'What are you up to, Tommy Pickford?'

'Mr Dixon!' the boy cried. He'd never been so pleased to see his teacher.

'What are you up to?' the teacher demanded.

'Please, sir,' Tommy gabbled. 'Marvello and Alice really did kidnap Laura, like I told you this afternoon.'

The teacher's eyes narrowed behind his glasses. 'Really?'

'Yes. But I took her place in the magic box and Laura escaped,' the boy went on.

'And then you escaped, did you?' Mr Dixon asked.

'Yes,' Tommy panted. 'And I locked the magician and Alice in the boiler room.'

'Did you, now?'

'Yes. You have to believe me this time, please, Mr Dixon!' Tommy pleaded.

'I believe you,' the teacher said slowly. 'And I think you've done really well.'

Mr Dixon had never told Tommy that he'd done well before. The boy's head was spinning. 'So are we going for the police?'

'Ah. We can use the phone in the school.'

'It's locked.'

'I have the keys,' the man explained and jangled them in his hand. He unlocked the main door to the school and smiled at the boy. 'There should be a reward in this for you.'

He led the way past the school office. 'Aren't you going to use the phone in the office?' Tommy asked.

'I want to get a look at these crooks first. Let the police know what they're up against,' the teacher explained as he hurried towards the boiler room.

'They may escape!' the boy gasped.

'They'll have to get past me first,' Mr Dixon

said grimly as he unlocked the door and threw it open.

Marvello was sitting on the box. Tommy saw the magician look up at the teacher – and a wide smile crossed the magician's thin face. 'Charles!' he said smoothly. 'You caught the boy. Well done.'

Tommy went weak at the knees. Too weak to turn and run. Too weak to struggle when the teacher turned and threw him into the room.

Mr Dixon closed the door and stood with his back to it. 'You've bungled everything, haven't you, brother?' he asked the magician. 'You let the girl escape, you collected a policeman and you even managed to let this scrap of a boy go.'

'We can always get the girl another day,' Marvello shrugged. Now that Tommy looked closely he could see how the magician looked very like the teacher.

'The girl knows who captured her,' Mr Dixon said. 'You'll have to stay under cover for a while. I'll think of another plan to get her next term.'

Marvello shook his head. 'She'll know you were in the plot. The boy will tell her.'

Mr Dixon smiled nastily. 'The boy is the only one who knows. All we have to do is let that dozy policeman go free, then deal with the boy.'

'You can't hurt the poor kid,' Alice put in.

Mr Dixon's eyes narrowed again. 'Take the policeman out to the street and let him go,' he ordered. He sounded like a classroom teacher again.

'Come along,' Alice said to the policeman, holding out her hand.

He held his hand out happily, singing, 'Here's my handle, here's my spout!'

Alice disappeared with P.C. Elloe.

'Now the boy can stay down here until we get the girl.'

'That could be weeks,' Marvello groaned.

'Let me worry about him,' the teacher said. 'Go out to the van and have the engine running ready for a quick escape.'

Marvello vanished up the stairs.

Mr Dixon locked the door and turned the key. He looked at Tommy. 'I'm going to try my own vanishing trick on you, Pickford. But this time you won't be appearing again ... ever!'

Chapter Ten
Boiler Bang, Blazer Burn

Mr Dixon looked at the boiler carefully. He muttered to himself, then turned a switch. There was a *whoosh!* as the gas jets lit. The teacher explained what he was doing.

'The gas heats the water in this boiler, you see?'

'Yes, sir,' Tommy said, blinking through his glasses.

'This pump sends the hot water into the radiators in the classrooms and that's what heats the school, you see?'

'Yes, Mr Dixon.'

'But, if we switch the pump off, then the water just stays in the boiler doesn't it?' the teacher said and he flicked the switch off.

'Yes, sir.'

'And the water boils and makes what?'

'Eh?'

'What does boiling water make?' the teacher snapped.

'Please sir, a cup of tea, sir!' Tommy answered.

Mr Dixon sighed and rubbed his eyes. 'No,

no, no! It makes steam. What does it make?'

'Steam, sir.'

'And when the steam can't get out of the boiler, then it bursts the boiler. There is a big explosion, isn't there?'

Tommy didn't answer this time. The water was already beginning to gurgle in the tank and the room was growing hot.

'I guess it will take just ten minutes, Pickford!' the man cried and sweat was running down his face. 'In ten minutes you will have hopped the twig!'

'Please, sir, I can't see any twigs.'

'You will have kicked the bucket! You will be in Kingdom Come!' the teacher screamed and his greasy grey hair was falling on to his damp forehead. 'Where will you be?'

'Please, sir, I'll be out in the school yard,' Tommy said.

'Ye-es!' the teacher roared. Then he blinked. 'Eh? You will be out in the school yard?' he croaked as the water hissed and bubbled angrily.

'Yes. Laura should be back with the police at any minute,' Tommy explained. The sweat on his nose was making his glasses slip down. He took them off to clean the steam off them.

'She doesn't know where we are!' the teacher snarled.

Tommy shrugged. 'She'll have seen when she

climbed out of the van,' he said.

The teacher's mouth fell open. Then he snapped it shut. 'In that case the accident will have to happen a little quicker!' He heaved at the stiff lever of the boiler till the gas roared. 'You haven't got ten minutes to live,' he snarled. 'You have only half that time. What is half of ten, boy?'

'Please, sir, twenty,' Tommy said.

'Twenty! *Twenty!* With pupils like you it's no wonder I'm desperate to get out of teaching!' The man wandered to the door, unlocked it and left, locking it behind him.

Tommy dashed towards the control lever. It was far too stiff for his matchstick arms to pull. He looked up at the pump switch. If he could turn that, then the pump would take away the boiling water.

He couldn't reach. The boiler was groaning and clanking now. The whole room seemed to be shaking. Tommy's shirt was sticking to his back with sweat as he dragged the magic box across to the control panel. He climbed on the box and reached up. His finger touched the switch but he couldn't grip it to turn it. The side of the boiler was so hot it was scorching him now.

Tommy jumped down and turned the box on to its edge. The extra few centimetres made the difference. As his thin blazer began to smoulder against the hot metal, he twisted the switch before falling backwards off the box.

The boiler was jumping and clattering like a runaway train. It gave no sign of cooling off. Tommy backed towards the door.

That was when Tommy Pickford's world exploded ...

* * *

Tommy woke up shivering. Everything was happening at once. A policeman was covering him with a blanket and saying, 'He'll be all right when we get him to hospital.'

Laura was bending over him and her hot tears were dripping on to his face as she moaned, 'Oh, wake up, Tommy. Tell me you're all right.'

Blue lights were flashing in the school playground and sirens were wailing as more police cars arrived.

'I'm all right,' he whispered and struggled to sit up. Every bone in his body seemed to ache but his head was worst of all.

A policeman in a battered helmet looked at him. 'Sorry about that, Tommy,' he said.

Laura put her arms around Tommy and pulled him towards her till he stopped shivering.

'Why? Why is the policeman sorry?' the boy asked weakly. 'It was Mr Dixon ... he ran away! He tried to kill me!'

'Let's get you into the ambulance, get you to hospital for a check-up, and then we'll explain,' P.C. Elloe said and picked Tommy up in his arms.

It was an hour before he was tucked into a warm hospital bed and found himself surrounded by people. Laura held his thin hand and explained.

'I got out of the van after Marvello carried you out in the magic box. I saw we were at the school and thought it would be best if I ran home and called the police from there. But I had problems.'

Mrs Lund blushed. 'It was such an incredible story – Laura's dad and I didn't believe her, I'm afraid,' she said.

'So I decided I had to go back and rescue you myself,' Laura said.

'But in the rush she dropped this letter,' Mr Lund put in. 'It was a ransom note. When we read that, we called the police at once.'

Laura took up the story. 'On the way back to the school I saw a policeman walking down Meek Street.'

'That was me,' P.C. Elloe said.

'I told him to follow me. There'd been a kidnap! He just said he was a little teapot!'

'It was that crack on the head,' the policeman said.

'So what did you do?' Tommy asked.

It was Laura's turn to blush now. 'I ... er ... took my shoe off. And I ... er, sort of reminded him who he was.'

'She cracked me over the head with the heel of the shoe,' the policeman said and rubbed his aching skull.

'It worked,' Laura said with a worried smile.

'It worked,' P.C. Elloe said.

'When we got to the school we saw Mr Dixon coming out and locking up,' Laura went on. 'Of course we didn't know that he was the boss of the gang. It was all his idea. He said he'd seen

Marvello's van drive off down the street. We thought we'd lost you again. But at that moment the van came back, Marvello leaned out and called to Mr Dixon to get in. Mr Dixon made a dash for the van but Constable Elloe stopped him.'

'Rugby tackle,' the policeman said proudly.

'Marvello got out of the van to help Mr Dixon ... so I nipped round to the driver's side and pinched the van keys. They couldn't get away!'

'But he blew me up!' Tommy said. 'How come I haven't hopped the bucket and kicked the twig?'

'I'm coming to that,' Laura promised.

Chapter Eleven
Bad Brothers, Warm Walk

'Mr Dixon started arguing with Mr Marvello ... it seems they are brothers,' P.C. Elloe said.

'I know,' Tommy nodded.

'Mr Dixon blamed Marvello and Marvello blamed you. That was when Mr Dixon said they wouldn't have to worry about you anymore. That you'd be dead within a minute. Marvello and the girl Alice went mad. They said they never meant to hurt anyone.'

'But Mr Dixon was laughing and going potty by then. He said the test scores for his class marks would be much better once you were dead,' P.C. Elloe said with a shake of his head.

'We only had about half a minute left by then,' Laura said and her eyes pricked with tears as she remembered. 'It took us that long to open the school doors. Alice told us where you were locked away – if we'd had to search the school it would have taken us half an hour to look there, not half a minute.'

'But the boiler exploded!' Tommy said. 'Why am I not dead.'

'It didn't explode,' the policeman said. 'You turned the switch that saved your life ... and saved the school as well. There'll be a very large reward for that! I think you'll have a pretty happy Christmas after all!'

'And there'll be an even bigger reward for saving Laura and my million pounds,' Mr Lund promised.

But Tommy wasn't interested in money at that moment. He was almost bouncing out of bed with the demand to know what had happened. 'I felt the explosion!'

The constable grinned. 'There wasn't time to open the door. I charged it with my shoulder and burst it open. I'm afraid you were standing behind it.'

'You weren't flattened by gallons of scalding steam. You were flattened by the door!' Laura laughed.

And Tommy grinned.

And P.C. L.O. Elloe chuckled.

And Mr and Mrs Lund smiled.

And, when Tommy's mother rushed into the hospital room to find her dying son, she found a room filled with people laughing till they cried.

* * *

Crisp, slow footsteps followed the children through the fog. They clicked against the damp pavement. A man in a dark suit with shining buttons was stalking the two friends.

They were too busy talking to notice. 'And our new teacher is Miss Gordon,' Laura explained. 'She's great. She'll have you reading in no time!'

Tommy nodded happily. The January day was bitter cold, but he was warm enough in his new coat, scarf and gloves, paid for by the rewards.

Then Tommy slowed and frowned. 'Aren't you still afraid, Laura?' he asked and looked around carefully. He thought he'd heard footsteps following them but he could have imagined it.

'Afraid?'

'Afraid they might try again!' he said.

'They'll be locked away for a long time,' Laura laughed.

'But there was the second woman – the one who was half of the sawn-up woman. The one who dressed like you and waved from the back of the hall. They never caught her! Maybe she'll try again.'

Laura shook her head. 'No, Tommy, I'm not afraid of her. Not when I have a hero like you to protect me.'

Tommy blushed. They set off again.

Soft footsteps followed the children through the fog.

'Hey, Tommy!' Laura said suddenly. 'Where did the policeman live?'

'Is this a joke?' the boy asked. He stopped and frowned at the damp pavement. The following footsteps stopped too.

'Yes,' the girl giggled. 'Where did the policeman live?'

'I don't know,' the boy shrugged.

'In the avenue!' Laura laughed.

Tommy blinked behind his glasses. 'Hah! Hah! Hah!' he laughed. 'That's very funny, Laura.'

Laura sighed. Sometimes telling jokes to Tommy Pickford was like stepping into a magic box – it got you nowhere. 'You're supposed to ask, which avenue.'

'Oh,' Tommy nodded. 'Which avenue?'

'In Hello-hello-hello Let's Be 'Avin-you!' Laura laughed. 'Get it? Let's Be 'Avin-you. Lettsby Avenue?'

The sharp footsteps took three quick strides towards the children and the tall man in the dark suit loomed out of the fog.

'That is not very funny,' Constable L.O. Elloe said and he scowled at them. 'Now get along to that school, you young villains, before I take you there in handcuffs!' he added with a twinkle in his eye.

As Tommy and Laura ran off laughing into the fog the policeman grinned and brushed the damp off his brand-new helmet.

He wandered down the road and as he chuckled his breath made clouds in the cold, damp air. 'Lettsby Avenue!' he giggled and set off for the police station for a warm cup of tea.

And soft footsteps followed the policeman through the fog ...

Look out for more

fantastic fiction in

Black Cats ...

TERRY DEARY
A Witch in Time

*Ellie sank on to the altar steps.
She wrapped her thin arms around the
black book. 'Perhaps they're right, then,'
she whispered. 'Perhaps I really am
a witch ...'*

Ellie and Sharon meet in the old
church. Sharon is hiding from the
school bullies, but Ellie is hiding
from a witchcraft trial – a trial from
six hundred years ago ...

SUE PURKISS
Spook School

What could be worse for a ghost
than not being spooky enough?

That's Spooker's problem as he faces his
all-important Practical Haunting exam.
It doesn't help that his task is to haunt
a brand new house – hardly the kind
of dark, dingy place where ghosts
are meant to dwell!

But when Spooker makes a new
friend, he might just find a solution
to his problems.

LYNDA WATERHOUSE
Drucilla and the Cracked Pot

Drucilla is famous for causing trouble –
but she isn't always to blame …

She didn't sell Pontius Maximus –
the Roman Army officer – a broken
pot, and it wasn't *her* toy chariot he
slipped on. It wasn't *her* idea for Mum
to get re-married and go back to Rome
to live. And as for finding the curse …

How does Drucilla cope with the
chaos and confusion of her life?

PHILIP WOODERSON
Moonmallow Smoothie

Sam's dad runs an ice cream parlour,
but his business is fast melting
away, thanks to competition from
Karbunkle's Mega Emporiums.

Then, suddenly one night,
a meteorite crashes to Earth in Sam's
garden. It's not just space-rock –
its special properties are perfect for
making ice cream. Soon everyone
wants a taste of Dad's latest invention,
called Moonmallow Smoothie.

But Sam's troubles are only
just beginning …

KAREN WALLACE
Something Slimy on Primrose Drive

When Pearl Wolfbane and her family
move into No. 34 Primrose Drive,
everything soon becomes murky, weird
and crumbling. Except for Pearl's room.
It stays pink, frilly and normal because
Pearl isn't like the rest of her family.

When Pearl meets her neighbours,
the Rigid-Smythes, she is delighted.
They have a swimming pool, not a
swamp; a kitchen, not a dungeon.

But they also have a daughter
called Ruby, and she isn't like her
family either …

Other titles available in Black Cats ...

Great stories for hungry readers